Ship's Cat
DORIS

About the author

Jane Simmons is best known for her award-winning books about Daisy the Duck, and her stories about Ebb and Flo, which were made into a television series. Jane lives on a boat, currently moored in Italy, with her very own cat named Doris! He has lived on the boat all his life, and loves travel, dogs, chickens and prawns. *Ship's Cat Doris* is Jane's second full-length novel, and follows the charming *Beryl Goes Wild*.

Jane says: "This is a story about when our cat, Doris, first came to live with us on our boat, *Prosperity*, along with John, Madge and Freda. We mended the boat with the help of many friends in Cornwall, and there was a cat called Jasper who Doris fought with. All the other characters in the book are fictional."

JANE SIMMONS

Ship's Cat
DORIS

ORCHARD BOOKS

ORCHARD BOOKS
338 Euston Road, London NW1 3BH
Orchard Books Australia
Level 17/207 Kent Street, Sydney, NSW 2000

First published in 2010 by Orchard Books
ISBN HB 978 1 408 308 950
ISBN PB 978 1 408 308 967

A CIP catalogue record for this book is available from the British Library.
1 3 5 7 9 10 8 6 4 2

Printed in the UK

Orchard Books is a division of Hachette Children's Books,
an Hachette UK company.

www.hachette.co.uk

CHAPTERS

BOSUN FINDS A KITTEN

It was a horrible stormy night. The little kittens snuggled up with Mummy Cat and listened to the thunder and lashing rain outside. The largest black and white kitten jostled with his brothers and sisters for the best and warmest position. He pushed his nose into the soft warm fur of Mummy's coat.

Shouting and screaming floated up the stairs. It had been going on all evening. It wasn't unusual – the family were loud and nasty, and they argued with each other all the time.

Hidden away in a cupboard on the landing, Mummy Cat had found the best place she could to protect her brood from the rough handling and loud voices of her violent owners.

"You'll be leaving soon," she said, nuzzling her kittens gently one by one. She had been through it all before and knew the time was coming. "You must be brave and make the best of your new homes." She gave them all a comforting lick.

The largest kitten snuggled up even closer to her and listened to the shouting and banging from below. He didn't like the family – they were rough with him. Just that morning he had been asleep when one of the children had grabbed him and started chucking him about. The woman had snatched him off the child, but she was no kinder and had thrown him into the air. He'd been terrified – one minute he was sleeping and the next he was flying through the air! He had managed to land without hurting himself, but as soon

as he touched the ground the woman had grabbed
him again, so he had bitten her as hard as he could
and fled back to Mummy Cat.

Suddenly the noises from below stopped. The
kittens heard someone coming through the front door.

"You'll be first, little one." Mummy Cat nuzzled the
largest kitten. "They always pick the biggest first, and

you bit the woman today." She hated losing her kittens, but she knew there was nothing she could do to stop it. She felt this tough little kitten had a better chance of surviving outside than any of her other babies, so she gently reassured him to help him on his way.

"Be brave, everything will be all right." She licked his face.

The kitten couldn't think of anywhere else he'd rather be. This was his whole world, tucked up with his brothers and sisters in Mummy's warm fur.

"I want to stay with you," he said, angry determination set on his tiny features.

Mummy Cat smiled at him, although the tiny frown broke her heart.

Suddenly, the airing-cupboard door was flung open. All the kittens tensed as one of the children appeared in the doorway and stared at them. They were all scared of the children.

"Get that big black and white one!" the woman shouted from below.

The child grabbed the largest kitten. Although he clung on as hard as he could, claws out, trying to stay with his brothers and sisters, the child was much too strong and easily lifted him free of the cupboard.

"Mummy!" he screamed in panic, all the time clawing to get back. But the cupboard door slammed shut and the child ran down the stairs, gripping tightly onto him with his sticky little hands.

He was passed from sticky hands to sweaty hands and then to rough-skinned gentle hands. He was lifted up and he looked into kind eyes peering out of a craggy, weather-worn face.

It was a gentle face that matched the gentle hand he was sitting in. The man's eyes twinkled softly with a kind humour and the kitten was calmed by his low soft voice. His panic subsided as his curiosity swelled and everything seemed to slow down. He blinked at the gentle face.

"This cat is definitely female?" Bosun asked the woman.

"Of course it's female!" the woman snapped. "She's as gentle as a butterfly," she added in a hissing whisper, flashing a sickly smile at Bosun.

"She's perfect!" beamed Bosun. "Are you going to be a good ratter, little cat?"

Bosun's smile lit up his whole face, and his twinkling eyes radiated warmth and kindness. The kitten relaxed into a bubble of safe tranquillity and purred.

Outside, the thundering storm was relentless. He curled up snugly in the chest pocket of Bosun's heavy coat and listened to the noise of the wind and the rain beating against the damp fabric.

The motion of Bosun walking rocked him in a gentle rhythm. He snuggled down, settled by the steamy warmth. Curling up into a tight ball, he shut his eyes and was comforted a little by the homely smell around him.

He was glad to be away from the frightening children, but he missed Mummy Cat already.

One minute he had been curled up in her soft fur with his brothers and sisters, the next, his whole family was gone and he was inside a dark, smelly pocket.

Suddenly, the kitten felt very lonely and anxious.

Where was he going? What would his new home be like?

ALL ABOARD
PROSPERITY

Bosun wound his way along the path which twisted down to the boatyard, and wondered if it was possible to get any wetter.

The Captain was waiting on the deck of their old wooden fishing boat, *Prosperity*. "Did you get the kitten?" she asked excitedly, looking eagerly at Bosun.

He nodded and clambered down the quay onto the deck beside her.

"You made sure it's a female kitten?" Cap asked.

"No doubt about it! She's lovely," beamed Bosun, as they all went into the warmth below decks.

From the moment Bosun's hand gently lifted him out of the damp pocket into the warm yellow glow of the cabin, the kitten felt at home. The cabin was scruffy and make-do, but the creaking of the timbers and the slopping of the rising tide against the hull sounded like a lullaby to his ears. Everything seemed to slow down here; nothing jarred – things just rolled and slurped. Up to this point his whole life had been hiding from the horrible family – tugged and thrown around by excitable children, or stepped on and kicked by clumsy people. For the first time in his brief life, there was an oasis of calm and peace.

So this is my new home… he thought.

Bosun held him up in his gentle hands. "Isn't she just perfect?" he said, passing the little kitten to Cap.

Cap looked into the kitten's tiny bright face. "We should call her Doris," she smiled.

Bosun nodded in agreement. "Yes…Doris."

Doris purred, comforted by the soft, round features of Cap's face, whose deep blue eyes shone with amusement. When she sat on the sofa, Doris snuggled up in her fluffy jumper and purred happily into the soft wool.

"Well, Doris, time you met your new brother and sister: Madge and John," Bosun said. He opened the bedroom door and two dogs bounded out excitedly into the centre of the cabin. They seemed to fill the space completely.

Doris panicked. His fur instinctively rose, and his whole body stiffened in shock. The dogs spied him immediately and, wide-eyed with excitement, lurched

towards him, sniffing and whining. They were so big – even the small one was enormous. They came very close to Doris, their noses huge and disgustingly wet. Doris's fur stood right up on end; he was stiff-legged and on tiptoes, his back arched. He spat and hissed at the dogs and they backed off a little.

"Madge! John! Give her some space!" Cap frowned at the dogs and wrapped Doris protectively in her smooth warm hands. He relaxed into her soft mohair jumper as she cuddled him. It reminded him of his mummy.

Little Madge and Big John sat down, but they didn't take their eyes off the newcomer for one second.

"Isn't she sweet!" sighed Cap. She stood up and

gently put him onto the galley tabletop and set a bowl
of warm milk in front of him.

Little Madge growled. "It's a cat!" she said in disbelief.
"They brought a cat in here!"

"But he's cute, isn't he?" said Big John with a
crooked smile. He peered up at Doris, his nose just
level with the work surface.

Madge was staring at Doris intently, her whole
body tense, just waiting for Doris to move.

"Madge loves to chase cats. It's her favourite game,"
explained John apologetically to Doris. Doris didn't
move a muscle.

"Go on, run!" said Madge and, not able to contain
her excitement any more, she started to jump up and
down on the spot. "You know you want to!"

"Leave the poor thing alone. Can't you see he's
frightened?" said John, frowning at Madge as she
leapt up and down.

Then he turned to Doris and said in a soft voice, "Take no notice of her, she won't hurt you." He had enormous kind eyes, like a gentle giant.

"Madge! Leave Doris alone!" Cap snapped. Madge grumbled and sat down, but she still couldn't take her eager eyes off Doris.

DORIS'S NEW HOME

Doris slept on the bed with Cap and Bosun. He listened for some time to make sure the dogs were fast asleep in the cabin, and even though all the night noises were strange to him, he slept more soundly than he had ever slept before. He felt safe with Bosun and Cap.

The next morning Doris woke
up at the bottom of their bed.
It took him a second to realise
where he was. There were
clucking and scratching noises
coming from the main cabin, but
he couldn't see what was making
them. The floor was a long way
from the bed. He slid down the
overhanging quilt backwards, his
sharp claws digging into the fabric,
and silently slipped onto the floor. He crept into the

main cabin to take a peek.
To his horror there was a
huge bird strutting about,
with an evil looking beak
and blood-red eyes.
Freda saw Doris
immediately. "Who are
you?" she squawked,
flapping her wings and

screeching in alarm. Chickens don't trust cats and Freda was no exception – she didn't like them one little bit. There was a cat in the boatyard who had tried to bite her a few times, and now there was one on her boat! She fluffed out her feathers to make herself look bigger, and stretched her neck up to show her full height.

John and Madge were stretched out asleep on the sofa, and they woke up at all the noise. "That's the new crew member. He came last night. Don't worry, he's only a little kitten." John yawned.

Freda relaxed as she noticed how small Doris was. "You're just a teeny weenie cat," she sneered as she looked at him sideways. She strutted over, confident now that she towered over Doris. Doris froze in terror. He'd never seen a bird before and this one was getting much too close for comfort.

As quick as a flash, Freda pecked his tail. Doris yowled in pain and dashed under the bed out of her way, hiding in the folds of some soft things that were stored under there. Luckily Freda was too big to follow him in. When he was sure he was safe, he relaxed and licked his tail where he had been pecked. It hadn't broken his skin, but it still hurt.

Not wanting to go back out to where the giant bird could get him again, he pushed his way through all the soft things and further into the darkness. At the back he found a small passage, and following it he came out into one of the cupboards in the main cabin. It seemed to be made for him and him alone to fit into.

He peeked through the slatted doors into the cabin and watched John, Madge and Freda from the

safety of his hidey-hole. He stayed there watching them until Cap and Bosun were up and about. Then he followed the passage further along and made his way through the twists and turns until it came out in the engine room, managing to bypass Freda and Madge in the main cabin.

"Doris!" called Cap. She held a bowl of cat food for his breakfast and she was surprised to see that he was already waiting on the engine box next to his food tray.

"Is that your name?" Freda squawked at Doris.

"What?" asked Madge, pricking up her ears. She even stopped eating her breakfast.

"They've called him Doris!" Freda explained, sniggering.

Madge spluttered out the mouthful of food she'd been chewing. "They can't do that, it's a female name!" she snorted. She didn't like things to be muddled up and she didn't like this boring little cat having anything to make him stand out. No. An interesting or even mysterious name like Doris just wouldn't do!

"I like it," said John, smiling at Doris.

"I reckon they think you're a she," Freda tilted her head and fixed Doris with a wicked glint in her eye. She felt even more superior to this little cat now. At least Freda was a proper name. At least Cap and Bosun knew she was female. They didn't even know whether the kitten was a girl or a boy!

"I don't mind," said Doris, and turned back to finish his breakfast. He really didn't mind. He was pleased John liked his name, but he couldn't care less what the others thought. He could feel Freda and Madge staring at him, but when he did look up again, he saw John smiling kindly at him.

As Doris settled in to his new home, Madge, John and Freda began to get used to having him around. Doris was so much smaller than any of them and the dogs were huge and clumsy. It was safer to try and keep out of their way.

Freda was harder to avoid. She was very excitable and would lie in wait to try to peck him whenever she got the chance. When she spotted him she'd shout, "Oi, Cat!" and chase him, stabbing at his tail. But after the first attack Doris was determined never to get pecked again! He was fast and *Prosperity* had lots of hiding places and secret passages that offered him a quick escape. Ducking and diving from Freda meant that he ended up exploring all the nooks and crannies of the old fishing boat.

The more Doris explored, the more it seemed as though the whole of the boat had been specially made for a cat. There were so many passages, and Doris found he could go from the front of the boat to the back without ever having to come out into the cabin. Wriggling between the inner and outer hull and under the floor, he'd sneak through cupboards and behind shelves. But his favourite place by far was under the bed. Doris squeezed between all the soft and hard odds and ends that were stowed under there. He made a cosy den for himself so he could hide from everyone, but especially from Freda and her sharp beak.

When eventually Doris felt he had sussed out the basic layout of the boat, his attention started to turn to the outside. He tried to climb the stairs up into the wheelhouse, but the gaps between the wooden steps were enormous.

He could only just reach the first one, and by digging his claws into the wood he managed to haul

himself onto the next. By the time he clawed his way up a few steps, he was exhausted and was still only halfway up. Puffing and panting, he looked up and his heart sank. At the top of the stairs was bright-eyed Freda, lying in wait for him.

"Oi, CAT!" she squawked.

Next he tried the porthole in the galley. When the deck was clear, he hopped out, ran along the deck as fast as he could and hid behind some

ropes that were tied up in loops.
Peeking through the coils of rope,
he could see the others lazing
about in the sun.

Freda had settled on the
cabin roof, luckily with her
back to him. Now he was out, he felt excited. From
his hiding place he could see most of the boat. The
quay loomed above him, but he couldn't see what was
up at the top and beyond. He jumped up onto the
bulwarks, but all he could see was the quay wall. It
was made of soft wood. Doris sank his front claws
into it. It oozed smelly seawater from behind
clinging weed.

It was horrible, but
Doris was so curious to
see what was at the top,
he wrinkled his nose at
the smell and the slime
and started to claw his
way up.

Although it was slow going, he was doing surprisingly well, and he became more excited with every step. Then Freda squawked behind him. The hair on Doris's back stood up as he helplessly clung onto the slimy wall.

"Oi, Cat!" Freda yelled. Doris froze. He wasn't far enough up to be out of pecking range, so he only had one choice: to go back down and inside before she could get him. He jumped back onto the bulwarks and Freda started across the cabin roof towards him.

Doris sprinted down the deck as fast as his little legs would carry him. Freda was right above him striding along the cabin roof. He sped around the corner and Freda leapt off the roof flapping in the air directly above him, her squawking vibrating through his bones. He shut his eyes and leapt as fast as he could through the galley porthole just as Freda landed on the deck, brushing him with her outstretched claw.

"Oi, Cat!" Freda yelled, trying to force her way through the porthole, but Doris was safe on the galley tabletop. He'd outrun her!

"My name is Doris!" he said firmly. He watched Freda poke her head through the porthole, squeezing and squeezing, but it was too small for a chicken.

Doris purred.

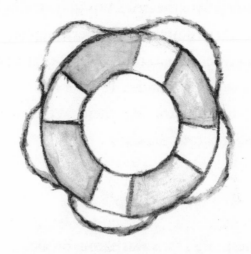

A STRANGE SMELL

Doris spent the rest of the day mooching about in the passages and cupboards. It wasn't long before he noticed a weird, overpowering smell. He could smell fish in a few corners, and wood rot in some of the ship's timbers, but the smell that puzzled him was something else: something alive...

He could smell it in the bilges and under the bunks, on the shelves and even on the deck. Doris could smell it all over the boat. Behind the galley he found a place where the smell was very strong. There were lots of chewed up bits of paper and cloth, all gathered together into a corner. Doris noticed fur lined a hollow in the bundle. It was a nest! Doris wondered what creature slept there. Why hadn't he seen it? Was it part of the crew?

The next morning Doris was eating breakfast when his questions were answered. There was an almighty crash in the galley as something smashed onto the floor. Cap let out a yell.

Madge was first on the scene. "It's a rat! It's a rat!" she barked excitedly.

"A rat?" said John, looking puzzled.

"A RAT!" squawked Freda in alarm. Freda was scared stiff of rats.

"Yeah! A RAT!" Madge shouted with the sheer excitement of it all, spinning on the spot, hardly able to contain her glee.

"Is that good?" Doris asked John as he came to sit next to him. He felt safe with John.

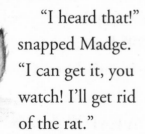

"Madge likes chasing rats, but she never catches them," he whispered. "They hide where she can't get them."

"I heard that!" snapped Madge. "I can get it, you watch! I'll get rid of the rat."

"Oh yes, please get rid of it!" implored Freda.

John tutted and rolled his eyes to the sky.

"Do they smell?" asked Doris, suddenly remembering the nest he had discovered yesterday.

"You're too small to catch a rat!" snorted Madge. "Leave it to the expert and don't get in my way!" she added, pushing her face right into Doris's.

John tutted again.

"I hate rats. They're so disgusting!" frowned Cap. She was standing in the galley holding a loaf of bread. The middle of it had been eaten away so it was just an empty crust. The end was smeared with dirt from where the rat had pushed its way in and dug out the soft centre.

"I only bought that this morning!" cried Bosun as he gawped unhappily at the empty loaf.

"Well, that's our lunch gone," grumbled Cap, throwing the remains into the bin. "I'll have to go through all the food cupboards to see what else the rat has got its teeth into."

Bosun looked hopefully at Doris. Such a small kitten – it could be months before she'd be ready to get rid of rats for them.

"One day, eh, Doris? One day," he said, giving Doris's head a gentle stroke. Then he followed Cap back into the galley to find out  what other horrid things the rat had done.

Doris sniffed the loaf in the bin. It was definitely the same smell as the one he'd detected yesterday.

He crept under the floor behind the galley.

Squatting down, Doris hid in a dark corner, with a view of the nest on one side and some passages on the other.

Doris had never seen a rat before, so he didn't know what one looked like. He hunched in the dark, eyes wide, every muscle taut, smelling all the different smells that wafted past and hearing every sound, however tiny and distant.

His whiskers were as stiff as wire, sensing any vibration in the air.

Although Doris was very small and young, the ratting instinct that pumped though his veins had been passed down through his parents and their parents and all of his ancestors. He was a ratter, born and bred.

Something scurried in the distance, snuffling and sniffing along the passage.

Doris couldn't see it yet, but it was something big and it was getting nearer...

Shifting haunches, Doris's eyes fixed on the space

where it would emerge, his muscles tense and poised ready to pounce.

Snuffle, snuffle, sniff… A large, twitching nose appeared in the opening…and Doris struck!

DORIS THE RATTER

The rat squealed. Doris squealed! The rat was enormous. It twisted and lunged, baring its huge teeth at him, but its mouth couldn't reach Doris because he had it wedged with a paw on either side of its head. Doris clung on, more from sheer terror than anything else – the rat was so much bigger than he had ever imagined.

The rat took off down the passage, Doris clinging

onto its back like a jockey on a horse. They shot out
of a cupboard and across the cabin floor. Cap yelled
and Bosun whooped. John barked, Freda squawked
and Madge leapt after them, but the rat dived under
the bed before she could reach them.

No matter how hard he tried, the rat couldn't shake
Doris off. He ran through narrow gaps and low gaps,
but Doris's fear helped sink his claws deeper into the
rat's back. The rat burst
out of the stowage area
and raced back across the
cabin floor.

Bosun gasped and Cap
stared open-mouthed.
John barked, Freda screeched and Madge leapt after
them again, as the rat frantically raced up the stairs
and into the wheelhouse. Doris and the rat went out
the door and crossed the deck, and with all the
strength that he had left, the rat leapt into the air and
over the bulwarks towards freedom. At that moment,
Doris suddenly found the courage to let go.

He landed back on the deck just in time to see the rat dive into the green slopping sea and swim off as fast as it could.

Madge arrived panting by his side. "Beginners' luck!" she snorted.

"Yeah! You showed him!" squawked Freda excitedly. She looked over the side of the boat. "And don't come back!" she shouted.

"Doris the ratter! You're a proper ship's cat, Doris!" beamed Bosun as he swept Doris up into his arms. "You're no butterfly, that's for sure! Have I got a treat for you!"

"I've got some lovely milk!" smiled Cap.

"She doesn't want milk!" grimaced Bosun. "No one in their right mind wants milk!"

"She likes milk – you're the one who doesn't," said Cap.

"I've got something she'll really like – something special for a champion ratter, to keep her strength up!" grinned Bosun, carrying Doris below into the galley.

Madge watched Bosun take Doris down the stairs, his face beaming with delight and pride, hugging Doris so tightly they seemed to become one. She growled a low growl, narrowing her eyes. She'd never seen Bosun go all gooey over anything before, let alone some little pipsqueak!

 Doris looked at the pink things in the bowl. They smelt good, sort of fishy and sweet. They tasted delicious, too! He purred.

Freda cooed from the cabin. "You're so brave!" she gushed. "Thank you so much, Doris."

Freda had been terrified of rats since the time she'd lived on a farm. Rats would break in to the chicken coop to steal the eggs and they'd bite any chicken in their way. She'd even seen them kill chicks. Seeing Doris's courage in getting rid of that rat had completely changed her mind about him. Doris was Freda's hero.

The Captain came with a bowl of milk. When she saw Doris, she froze.

"My prawns! You've given that cat our dinner!" cried Cap.

"Yeah, but the rats won't be eating our lunch again!" smiled Bosun. "A champion's dinner for a champion ratter!"

They both watched Doris finish the special treat.

"I'm glad the vet's coming in the morning. Rats are such dirty creatures – they carry all sorts of disease." Cap looked worried.

"She didn't even get a scratch," Bosun reassured her.

"All the same, I'll feel happier when the vet has checked her over," said Cap, giving Doris a stroke.

Doris didn't feel at all like a hero. As he gobbled up his prawns he was just relieved the whole rat episode was over. Gradually his heart slowed to a normal pace and his panic and fear faded.

He could see Madge glowering at him. He decided not to admit that he had only clung on to the rat because he was too frightened to let go. When Cap stroked him, he saw Madge scowling at him more than ever. He blinked and purred as loud as his lungs would let him.

THE BEAST VISITS

When the vet entered the boatyard, Freda came running as fast as she could.

"The Beast! The Beast! The Beast!" She screeched the alarm the whole way from the gate.

Madge and John disappeared immediately as if by magic. By the time the vet knocked on the boat, only Doris, Bosun and Cap were left in the cabin. None of the others were anywhere to be seen – none of them wanted to see the Beast and, more importantly, they didn't want the Beast to see them.

Doris heard Freda's alarm, but he didn't know what it meant. He only realised that everyone else had disappeared when the vet was already in the cabin.

"She really is a wonderful ratter!" grinned Bosun. "She takes her job very seriously."

"Glad to hear it," said the vet. "Now, let's have a look at you Doris."

The first part of Doris's check-up went very well. The Beast examined him all over: teeth, paws, heartbeat, ears and eyes. Doris didn't mind at all – he quite enjoyed all the attention. *Why have all the others disappeared?* he wondered. Doris liked the vet a lot. She was very friendly and gentle. He began to purr.

Then, the second part of his check-up began. Although the vet kept talking gently and stroking and reassuring Doris, she was also sticking needles and thermometers into him at the same time. It was horrible!

If only I'd hidden with the others, he thought miserably.

Doris was still terribly shocked when all of a sudden the vet picked him up and held him upside down. Cap and Bosun gathered round and they all stared at his underneath. Doris looked pleadingly at Bosun, but everyone was in deep discussions about something, and then it was all over and Bosun and Cap laughed. Bosun picked Doris up and gave him a tight hug. Doris purred.

Later that evening, when the vet had gone, Madge, John and Freda came out of hiding.

"You should have hidden like I told you to!" Freda whispered to Doris.

"You didn't!" Doris said.

"Yes I did, I yelled all the way from the gate that the Beast was coming," Freda protested.

"Yeah, but you didn't say to hide!" Doris groaned.

"Oh," said Freda, frowning. "I thought you'd know that. Sorry."

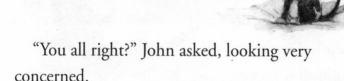

"You all right?" John asked, looking very concerned.

"Yeah," said Doris. Then something awful occurred to him. "Does the Beast come often?"

"Every week!" said John.

Doris froze.

John chuckled. "Only teasing! It'll be ages before she comes again."

Doris felt a wave of relief wash over him. He didn't want to go through that again in a hurry!

Cap and Bosun huddled over the table under the
yellow glow of the paraffin lamp, talking very softly so
Doris wouldn't hear.

"How could we have been so stupid?" said Cap.
"Do you think we can still call him Doris?"

Bosun looked across at Doris who was licking the
last of his dinner off his plate. He leant over the table
towards Cap. "It kinda suits him, and I've got used to
it now," he whispered thoughtfully.

Cap took a long look at their ship's cat, Doris. Doris blinked back at her with a satisfied, peaceful expression. It struck Cap how male he looked. How could they have thought he was a she?

"It's strange," Cap said, "but I know exactly what you mean. He can't be called anything else. He's Ship's Cat Doris, and no other name will do!"

MADGE AND THE CRABS

Soon Doris had found a little routine of his own.
During the day he would sleep, then get up and eat
his dinner. During the night he would jump ship and
creep around the boatyard. By morning he was always
back on the boat, ready for his breakfast, before taking
a nice long sleep, sometimes under the bed and
sometimes in the wheelhouse.

He grew bigger and stronger every day. Getting up

onto the quay and back became easier and easier. When Doris came back in the early hours of the morning, John would be sitting as still as a statue on the deck. He always winked at Doris and Doris felt extra safe when he saw him there. Madge was a different kettle of fish. If she saw him she would chase him down the deck.

One morning, Madge sat on the deck and watched Doris. She thought he was slinking across the boatyard as though the place belonged to him. She still didn't like him. He was just never around long enough to try. It seemed to Madge that Doris only had to turn up at meal times and he always got a kiss or stroke from Bosun or Cap. She'd seen them treating him like a hero, as though he had just crossed the Atlantic or walked to the North Pole, cooing over him and giving him treats. Madge hung out with John. They played, ate and slept together, and even Freda

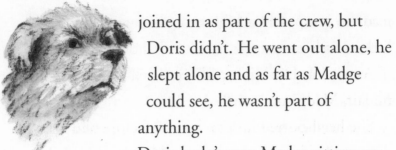

joined in as part of the crew, but
Doris didn't. He went out alone, he
slept alone and as far as Madge
could see, he wasn't part of
anything.

Doris hadn't seen Madge sitting on
the deck, and before he got too close, she sneaked out
of sight around the corner and
waited for him.

Doris trotted up to
Prosperity. He'd had a lovely
time playing in the shadows
and had really worked up an
appetite. He licked his lips at
the thought of his breakfast.
The tide was out, so it was
quite a leap down onto the
deck. He stood on the
quayside to judge the distance.

Madge hid behind the
wheelhouse, watching him get

ready to jump. It was high time she taught this spoilt little cat a lesson.

As soon as Doris jumped off the quay and was in midair, Madge pounced!

She head-butted him on his side before he'd even dropped halfway to the deck, and knocked him clean over the side of the boat. Doris howled as he plummeted down between the quay and the boat. He grabbed at the wall and luckily his claws sank into the soft wood. Madge growled down at him as he peered up the dark gap.

Doris started to claw his way up the slimy wall, but to his horror things started popping out of all the cracks. *Snip! Snip! Snip!* In no time at all, the whole wall seemed to be moving. Crabs!

"What do you want?" cried the crabs. "Get off our wall!"

"That's what I'm trying to do!" wailed Doris, but the crabs weren't listening. They snipped their claws at him threateningly.

Doris struggled up the wall surrounded by the mob of crabs, trying not to get pinched by their huge pincers. When he finally got to the top, Madge was waiting for him.

"You're not coming up!" Madge growled and nipped his ears when he got within reach. The sea slurped menacingly below as the tide flooded in.

"Please let me up!" Doris begged, but Madge had him trapped. Her wrinkled nose and nasty grin told Doris he was in serious trouble.

The crabs closed in on him shouting, "In the sea! In the sea!" and nipped at him with their sharp pincers. Just as Doris started to despair that he couldn't hold on any longer, a large shadow fell across them all.

"Let him be!" The command came like a roll of thunder. John towered above them.

Madge stopped immediately, hung her head and retreated inside.

Doris was overjoyed to see John. He hauled himself up and shook the last crab off his tail as he flopped onto the deck exhausted.

"Crab! I'll get it!" shouted Freda, and chased the snipping creature down the deck. Doris watched her, still catching his breath.

"She loves eating them," John said. "Are you OK?"

"Yeah," said Doris. But he wasn't really.

Madge curled up on the sofa, sulking. She watched as Doris nipped down the stairs and ate his breakfast as though nothing had happened. She couldn't believe how close she'd been to giving that little squirt a dunking in the sea. John should mind his own business!

To add insult to injury, Doris curled up on Cap's lap, licking his lips in satisfaction and falling fast asleep, Cap stroking him all the while. Madge glared at him.

"What's the matter with you?" John asked.

"I hate that cat," grunted Madge.

"Well, I like him and even Freda likes him," John said quietly. "You'll get used to him."

"I don't want to get used to him!" frowned Madge.

"You used to feel that way about me, when I first came," said John.

"It's not the same!" Madge replied, and stalked off.

Doris dozed on Cap's knee. He couldn't care less what that stupid little dog thought of him.

Bosun, Cap, John and Freda liked him and that was the only thing that mattered.

John came over and nuzzled him.

"She doesn't mean it," he said gently. "She doesn't like anyone to begin with. I think it's because she was so badly hurt before."

"What do you mean?" Doris asked sleepily.

"Before Bosun and Cap rescued her, she was with a family who were cruel to her," he whispered, looking around to make sure Madge was out of earshot. "She had a broken leg and cuts and bruises. Madge said she was kicked about by the children and beaten by the people. I think she can't trust anyone now, not until she knows them really well."

Doris looked across the cabin to where Madge was curled up on some cushions. Her grumpy little face scowled at everything around her. He knew what it was like to be scared of children and to be kicked about. *It must have been terrible for Madge*, he thought.

"Will she always be nasty?" Doris asked.

"I think so. She's too old to change now," John said quietly, following Doris's gaze. "But she has a really nice side, too." Then, after a long pause he added, "She really has!" He winked at Doris and went out to sit on the deck.

FREDA GOES FOR
A SPLASH

Whenever the tide was out, Bosun was busy under the
boat, banging in nails or caulking between the planks
to stop the hull leaking. Cap usually worked inside or
was away, out of the yard. They would stop for tea
breaks and sit on the back deck with Doris, John,
Madge and Freda. Often Bosun would sigh – a sort
of sigh that was a mixture of exhaustion and
hopelessness, as if he couldn't get up again. But after

his coffee and biscuits he would manage to get up and start hammering all over again.

Doris noticed that Freda was always off around the boatyard, ready to help anybody who couldn't eat all their food. Straight after breakfast she would go to sit on the desk in the boatyard boss's office and coo at him. It was the perfect place for her to see who was in the yard for lunch. The boss always chatted away to her, passing her bits of toast now and again. All the people in the boatyard would go to the office first thing in the morning, to pick up their mail or check if they had any messages, and then Freda would follow them back to their boat. Everyone liked Freda and always gave her a biscuit or a bit of their sandwich. Doris would often spot Freda eating lunch with a sailor or sharing a bun with the crane driver. It seemed as if Freda knew everyone in the yard. The only time Freda came back to the boat was for more food at tea breaks, lunch and dinner. Freda knew she would always get a biscuit or a piece of something left over.

On one of their tea breaks, the sun was shining and Bosun had just come up from under the boat because the tide was coming in and the ground was getting wet underfoot. John and Madge were queuing up for a biscuit and Freda was doing a tightrope walk along one of the ropes that tied the boat along the quay. She was always doing that, even though she wasn't very good at it. She had her eyes firmly fixed on the biscuit tin and was excitedly skipping along.

"Biscuit time! Biscuit time!" she sang happily as she bounced along the rope.

"Sometimes I think we've taken on too much with this old boat, Cap," Bosun said, looking across the estuary.

"It'll take some time to fix up, that's for sure, but it will be worth it in the end," reassured Cap. "How's the hull coming along?"

"Slowly," sighed Bosun. "I think it'll have to come out of the water for me to mend it properly. There just isn't enough time between the tides to do a proper job."

"I hate being stranded on the dry," grumped Cap. She felt impatient and dreamt of a boat that just worked, so they could travel wherever they wished. "Boats are for bobbing about on the water. It's bad enough being stuck on the quay."

"One day," Bosun smiled, "*Prosperity* will be ready and we'll chug off to wherever we want…but not yet."

Just at that moment there was a squawk and a splash. Everyone jumped up and looked over the side to see Freda, wings outstretched, wallowing in the water. John and Madge barked and barked.

"Freda!" cried Cap. Bosun jumped down onto the quay and scooped Freda out of the sea as quick as a flash. He plopped the sodden chicken down on the deck and clambered over the bulwarks.

Cap wrapped Freda up in a towel and hugged her close to her chest.

"Oh, Freda!" Cap breathed, worry lines etched across her face. "What if we hadn't been here? You must be more careful!"

They took her down below. Doris padded downstairs to see poor wet Freda inside the oven with the door open, wrapped up in a towel.

"I'm freezing!" cried Freda shivering violently.

"It must have been horrible in all that water," said Doris, shivering just at the thought of it. "I hate water!"

"Me too," trembled Freda.

As Doris watched her dry out, Cap and Bosun huddled together, whispering.

"She's not very good at getting on and off the boat now we're not on the river anymore," said Cap.

"It's so different here, and the tides make it much more dangerous," sighed Bosun.

They decided that Freda should be penned up so she couldn't fall in the sea again.

Bosun spent the afternoon making a wooden hut, and by evening it was ready. Freda was dry and had recovered from her dunking.

Cap and Bosun put a mesh tent over the top of the whole cabin and placed Freda and her new hut inside it.

"You have to live here now because it's safer," Cap told Freda firmly. She brought her some food and water. Freda settled into her cosy hut and slept soundly, right through the night.

In the days that followed, it didn't go so well.

Freda wouldn't squawk or coo when Bosun and Cap were around. She didn't seem to be interested in anything. Bosun and Cap took their breaks with Freda and chatted to her through the mesh, but she didn't seem to know they were even there.

"She doesn't like being locked up," said Bosun, peering at her. "I don't blame her. I know I wouldn't like it."

"She'll get used to it," said Cap, hopefully.

That night, Doris and John sat next to Freda's home to talk to her.

"I hate it in here!" Freda yelled.

"But you keep falling in the water," Doris explained.

"I don't do it on purpose!" snapped Freda. "I can't get used to the boat."

"How come? Haven't you always lived here?" Doris asked.

"No!" shouted Freda. "I hate it in here!"

"We only moved onto this boat just before you arrived, Doris," John explained. "Before, we lived on a smaller boat, on the river. It was easier to get on and off."

"I don't understand the sea. It keeps coming and going!" cried Freda.

"So this is new for all of you?" said Doris, realising for the first time that it wasn't just him settling into a new home.

"I hate it in here!" Freda squawked again. "It's like it was on the farm – always in a cage!"

"In a cage?" asked Doris.

"Yes, thousands of us stuffed in little cages. It was horrible. Then Cap and Bosun saved me, but now I'm in another cage!" wailed Freda.

"If you keep falling in the water, you'll drown," John explained. "It's to keep you safe."

"I don't want to be safe! I hate it in here! I need to be free!" Freda cried. Suddenly she stopped and frowned. She looked straight at Doris, determination in her red eyes. In a low controlled voice she said, "I'm going on hunger strike until they let me out."

John tutted and raised his eyes to the stars.

Over the next few days Freda was true to her word
and didn't eat a grain of her food. She became thinner
and thinner.

"I hate seeing her like this," said Cap one day,
peering in at the sad-looking chicken. "She won't eat,
and she's even stopped laying eggs."

Bosun nodded sadly in agreement.

That afternoon, John and Doris sat with poor thin
Freda.

"Freda, are you OK?" asked John. He looked very
worried.

Freda didn't answer; not even a coo.

"We have to get her out of there," said Doris.

John started to object, but found that he couldn't

when he looked at Freda again.

"She needs her freedom, even if it's dangerous," said Doris firmly.

John knew in his heart that Doris was right.

Doris pulled at a corner of the mesh, tugging at it with his claws, and it started to come away from where it was fixed to the cabin roof. As soon as the corner lifted it was like opening a zip. At first Freda didn't notice, but when Doris poked his head through the opening he'd made and whispered her name, Freda jumped up, all excited. She was quickly back to her old self. After gobbling down her food she leapt through the hole and skipped around the deck, squawking and pecking at everything.

She ran up to
Doris, eyes shining
with delight.
"Thanks!" she
squawked, and then
she was off across
the yard to see all
the people

she had missed over the past few days.

Doris was stunned at Freda's instant
recovery and looked at John in utter
amazement. John tutted and rolled
his eyes.

When Bosun saw Freda skipping
about free, the change in her said it all. "Cap, come
and see this!" he called. They both smiled as the old
Freda scampered around the yard. Neither of them
had the heart to put her back in her enclosure.

Freda was happy again, so everyone else was happy. Luckily, on the odd occasions she fell into the water, Bosun or Cap were there to fish her out. Even though they would worry over her dripping body, wrapping her up and towelling her dry, they never even mentioned putting her back into the cage during the day. One time she managed to struggle out of the water herself. She got up onto one of the tyres hanging off the side of the boat and cooed until Cap heard her.

"Oh, Freda! What are we going to do with you?" said Cap in despair as she plucked Freda out of the tyre. Freda got quite used to sitting in the oven to dry out and even looked forward to it. At night Freda went back into her enclosure until morning. She didn't mind that, but she'd be ready first thing, scratching to get out as soon as there was someone about to keep an eye on her.

Bosun spent most of his time either hammering things onto the boat or pulling things off. Cap was clearing out everything they didn't want from the inside, which seemed to take forever.

John kept guard on the deck and Doris watched as everyone hurried about. It was as though everyone was getting ready for something. Doris wondered what it might be…

JASPER

Doris watched the comings and goings, but often he'd fall asleep until dinnertime. It was at night-time, when everyone else was asleep, that Doris was busy.

One night he was playing in a tarpaulin draped over a dinghy near *Prosperity*, when he thought he sensed something. He stopped playing and listened, but before he heard anything, a huge cat loomed out of the darkness and lunged at him.

Doris froze in alarm as the enormous creature flew through the air straight at him. Within a heartbeat, he pulled himself together and fled.

He ran as fast as his legs would carry him to the safety of *Prosperity*, but as he landed on the bulwarks, nearly home safe, he heard the gigantic cat hiss right behind him. An enormous paw caught him on the back and sent his rear end sideways.

Doris winced in agony as he felt the skin on his leg rip open. The power of the blow nearly knocked him off the side of the boat, but Doris clung on desperately. With all the strength he could muster, he clawed his body up and over the bulwarks and fell onto the deck. But he didn't even have time to catch his breath before the monstrous white cat was on top of him.

Pinning Doris to the floor, the cat hissed and spat, showing off his gleaming white teeth. Doris was more terrified than he had ever been before. Staring at those long sharp fangs so close to his face, he realised he could die here. He was completely outmatched – this cat could do whatever he wanted and Doris was powerless to stop him.

The white cat stretched up and, with his full force, bashed Doris square across his ear. For a brief moment Doris couldn't hear a thing past the ringing of his throbbing ear. Panicking, he desperately wriggled and wriggled, but he just couldn't free himself from the stocky cat's grip.

"This is my yard, so keep out of it!" The cat hissed rotten fish breath into Doris's face. Doris could feel himself shaking from nose to tail. The huge cat glared down his nose at him; he looked at Doris as if he was more disgusting than something he had to scrape off the bottom of his paw.

"If you think this is your yard, your family, your home – you're a stupid little idiot!" the huge cat sneered. "They'll leave you behind. That's what happens to cats – didn't anyone tell you? But this is my yard, dummy, and you're not staying here!" he spat. He bashed Doris again around his ear. It was like being hit by a brick. Doris's ears rang. He couldn't hear a thing.

Doris cried out as loud as he could, knowing his life depended on it. The sound of hurried footsteps on wood and Freda squawking and flapping in her cage made the huge cat release his grip and leap over the bulwarks.

With a yowl, the cat disappeared into the night.
Madge stood where the cat had been, a tuft of white
fur sprouting out of one side of her mouth. She was
rigid, nose wrinkled, exposing her sharp fangs, and her
flashing eyes were fixed on the disappearing cat. As
Doris's hearing returned, it was filled with Madge's
rumbling growl and Freda crying out, "Doris! Doris!
Doris!"

John arrived panting, out of breath. "Are you all
right?" he asked, looking anxiously at Doris.

"I think so," Doris replied shakily, licking the
wound on his leg.

"Who was that?" he asked, trying not to appear as frightened as he was.

"Jasper! I hate that posh cat more than I hate you," grunted Madge, spitting the fur out of her mouth and stomping back into the boat.

"Thanks," Doris said quietly to the retreating figure of Madge. He was still trembling and shuddered at the thought of what could have happened if Madge hadn't saved him.

"See, she likes you now," John whispered, winking at Doris.

"Really?" asked Doris.

"Believe me, that's as good as it gets," he smiled.

"I would've saved you!" Freda called out through the mesh. "If I wasn't stuck in here!"

"I know you would have," smiled Doris.

John tutted.

Curling up in the safety of the wheelhouse, Doris stared out across the yard. Flashes of lightning lit up the shadows, but he couldn't see Jasper. The wound on his leg throbbed and as he licked it he tried to empty his mind of the sneering poison Jasper had put there. What had he meant when he said they would leave him behind? This boat was his home, and Bosun, Cap, John, Freda and even Madge were his new family. *Weren't they?* He curled up tighter against the questions stirring in his mind and hated Jasper more than he had ever hated anyone.

OUT ON THE HARD

The rain and wind swept down the valley and kept everyone inside. Doris spent most of his time in the wheelhouse where he could keep an eye on the comings and goings of the boatyard. He was sitting watching the sun rise, when he noticed a large machine trundling down the yard towards the boat.

The machine parked just outside and belched smoke. The noise from it was horrible.

Doris didn't like it one little bit and disappeared down into the cabin to find his favourite place under the bed, where the noise and smell couldn't reach. He curled up and wondered how long it would take for the monster to go away.

"It's here!" shouted Cap excitedly. Bosun came to have a look.

"This is it, Cap. We'll be out this morning," Bosun said. They stood happily looking at the enormous crane, but it would be afternoon by the time *Prosperity* was ready to be lifted out.

Under the bed Doris tensed as the growling monster roared so loud it shook the whole cabin. Suddenly, the bed juddered and he clung on to the cushions surrounding him. His stomach lurched as he heard slurping and bubbling noises from below. The boat swung and all the cups and ornaments jingled on the shelves.

Now the roar of the monster was coming from directly below him. He curled up tightly, wishing it would stop. Everything jolted and juddered, and the whole boat shuddered; there were thumping and banging noises from all around the hull. Eventually the thumping stopped and Doris began to relax.

When the monster had gone, Doris crept out to see what had happened. The boat sat propped up on the hard surface of the yard like a beached whale. It was enormous out of the water and the deck was high up in the air. He could see over the rooftops of the houses behind the boatyard hedge. He had a bird's-eye view of the whole yard and the estuary beyond.

John and Madge were sniffing about in the yard and Freda was helping a sailor eat his afternoon bun. They looked so tiny from where Doris sat – even Bosun and Cap looked small.

Suddenly, a seagull swept just over Doris's head, screaming, "*Cat! Cat!*" It landed on a roof top behind the boatyard hedge. There were two of them making a nest on the edge of the roof. He watched as the two seagulls came and went all afternoon. Each time they swooped at him screaming, "*Cat! Cat!*", before depositing the twigs and leaves they'd brought to the roof to weave into their nest.

That evening, Bosun and Cap climbed a ladder to get on board. They lowered a big box over the side so John and Madge could be hoisted up. Freda flew up the ladder on her own. She did it one step at a time, flapping like mad on each rise, but she made it to the top safe and sound.

Doris was far too excited to eat his dinner. Even though the boat had moved only a few metres away from its berth on the quay, it felt as though everything had changed. He crept out on deck and peered over the side of the boat. It was a long way down; too far to jump. Freda sat in her hut chirping softly to herself. The mesh was gone and Freda was free to do what she pleased now they were safely out of the water.

That night, Doris was sitting on the bulwarks, looking down on the boatyard and wondering how he could get down, when he saw a white cat disappear into the shadows. Jasper! Doris limped slowly to the front of the boat, scanning the ground below for Jasper all the while.

When he reached the bows he sat and looked carefully at the shadows below. Doris thought he could just make out a tail twitching. He felt torn between wanting to go exploring and absolute terror of what would happen if Jasper caught him again.

He reasoned that at least he thought he knew where Jasper was, so he'd be safe if he could keep a good distance away from him. But all the same he trembled at the thought of Jasper even seeing him.

Silently, he leapt down onto a boat which was almost touching *Prosperity*. He found an easy way along the deck, keeping Jasper in sight, and slid to the ground. He crept along softly, staying in the shadows, sneaking to a safe place where he could keep an eye on Jasper. But when he looked at the place where he thought Jasper's tail had been twitching, it was gone! He could smell Jasper in the still night air, but to his horror, he couldn't see him anywhere.

Doris froze in the darkness. Where was Jasper? Doris looked to the far away safety of *Prosperity* and gulped. He stayed glued to the spot, not daring to move in case Jasper spotted him. After a while Jasper's scent faded, until he could no longer smell him at all, and he stood up carefully. He stared at *Prosperity*. Could he get back up there?

Nervously, Doris tried the ladder. By carefully jumping up each rung, he managed to get back on the boat easily. When he was at the top, he again scoured the yard below. When he was sure Jasper had gone, he tried going down again. It was a bit tricky, but he managed. Happy now he knew he could get on and off the boat, he sneaked around the area, checking out where he could hide and how quickly he could get back if Jasper did turn up. Feeling very pleased with himself and now sure that Jasper had gone, he started up the ladder as the light of dawn broke over the yard.

He was only halfway up when a seagull swooped out of the sky screaming, "*CAT! CAT!*" It dived. Doris froze, and the seagull grabbed at him as it swooped past, knocking

him sideways off the ladder. Doris frantically paddled the air and just caught hold of a rung. As soon as he landed, he leapt up to the safety of the boat, his heart pounding.

"Cat!" shouted the gull from high above. Doris glared at it. He was beginning to really hate the gulls. He licked his back where the bird had caught him. After his heart had slowed to a gentler pace, he went in search of his breakfast. Having eaten every last scrap, he stretched out in the wheelhouse just in time to hear everyone getting up in the cabin. Cap called him and gave him a stroke and a kiss on his head. Madge growled.

THE REAL WORK BEGINS

Doris curled up in the soft things under the bed for a good day's sleep.

Chippy the carpenter arrived just after breakfast. Cap and the dogs went out for the day. Freda had disappeared into the boatyard office to chirp and chatter with the boss, and to see who was about and what they might be eating.

Doris had just shut his eyes when a series of

banging and thudding noises came from the cabin, accompanied by the sound of splitting wood, as if something or somebody was tearing the whole boat apart. He lay there, tense, listening and trying to figure out what it could possibly be. The noise went on for ages, then as suddenly as it had started, it stopped.

Doris crawled out from under the bed. Everything was quiet in the cabin. He stood and stared at the hollowed-out shell in front of him. There was no floor, no seats and no galley. It was just the boat with all its ribs and hull exposed. All the comfort and softness had gone – it was dark and dirty. All Doris's secret passages were open and bare. He gaped at it. There was nowhere left for him to hide, nowhere left that was his and his alone. It was as though the whole of the boat's insides had been sucked out. Someone had taken his home away.

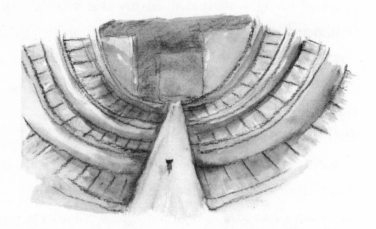

Doris cautiously crept through the empty carcass onto the deck.

On the ground, Bosun and some men were furiously sawing wood and screwing planks together. Doris was desperate to find a quiet spot to fall asleep for the day. At that moment a seagull swooped out of the sky screaming, "*Cat! Cat!*"

Cursing the seagull, Doris leapt back inside and down into the hollowed-out cabin. He felt wretched picking his way back through the creepy space and crawled back under the bed where at least it was warm. He couldn't understand what was happening: suddenly his home had disappeared, and the only safe place left was under the bed. Everywhere else had been taken over. Eventually he managed to fall asleep, even when the banging and crashing started up again.

Doris woke to silence. He took another peek into the cabin. There were planks of wood, boxes and tools laying about everywhere. As hard as he tried, he couldn't remember how it had looked before the banging had started. Suddenly he missed the others. Where were they? Had everything gone forever? Is this what Jasper had meant? Had they left him behind? A growing sense of loneliness enveloped him as he sniffed at the wood and screws.

The cabin reminded him of an old shed he'd seen in the yard, full of rubbish with no one living there. His home had gone. Someone had destroyed it. He wondered where they'd taken it to. Soon misery made him sleepy, and once again he fell fast asleep under the bed.

When Doris woke this time, he heard everyone coming back. John and Madge were sitting in the middle of the cabin on a bright new floor. It glowed in the lamplight with a newness and smelt of freshly sawn wood.

John smiled at him, and even Madge looked happy in the bare cabin. Freda cooed from her new perch at the top of the stairs. Doris was so happy to see them again!

Even though the boat was almost empty and all his passages still lay open, Doris started to feel excited by the change. Cap and Bosun were laughing and the whole atmosphere in the cabin was happy. He sat with John and Madge and they all watched Cap prepare their dinner. Doris looked across at his old hidey-holes, no longer hidden, and realised he didn't need them anymore. Sitting with John and Madge he felt part of it all, part of the crew. They hadn't gone away after all. He noticed how Madge was tiny and how John was so big and so gentle. While tucking into his dinner he purred and purred.

Things were getting better on *Prosperity*. It was clean and bright, it smelt good and, somehow, felt even safer.

THE SEAGULLS ATTACK

Doris was sitting on the bows scouring the yard for
Jasper, when he saw Bosun, John, Madge and Chippy
the carpenter picking their way along the path back
towards the boatyard. They turned the last corner and
were strolling across the car park, just before nipping
through the hedge, when John let out a bark. He
galloped over to the building where Doris had
watched the seagulls build a nest. He was nuzzling

something on the ground. Bosun, Madge and Chippy joined him. Doris could just make out a fluffy plump seagull chick.

"Oh dear, we'll have to put it back," said Bosun, looking down at the chick who was screeching and chirping. Bosun scratched his head and then squinted into the sun, trying to see all the way up to the nest on the roof.

"You have to be careful when it comes to seagulls," said Chippy, shaking his head. "My cousin got into bother with one once."

"We can't leave it here, though. It will die," said Bosun, looking back down at the poor little chick.

"You're right," said Chippy, frowning, and he went through the hedge to fetch the ladder. As soon as they had propped the ladder against the roof, Bosun climbed up with the squawking chick tucked under his arm. Soon he was level with the nest.

Doris anxiously watched Bosun reach the nest and pop the chick back with its shrieking brothers and sisters. But just then, a seagull swooped out of the sky and nearly swept him off the bulwarks. "*Cat! Cat!*" it screamed. Doris ducked and when he looked again, the seagull was swooping at Bosun, screaming, "Get off my babies!" Then it was joined by another and they both dive-bombed Bosun.

"Leave our babies alone!" they yelled as they dived and pecked at him. John and Madge barked and barked, trying to scare the seagulls away. Bosun scrambled down the ladder and in one movement swung it over his back. The others dived under it and used it as a shield. They fled as fast as they could through the gap in the hedge. John and Madge snapped and barked at the gulls. The angry birds flew over the hedge and attacked them on the other side as they ran through the boatyard, diving and pecking at them relentlessly.

Bosun and the others threw themselves under the boat. The birds swooped and dived, but couldn't get to them.

Doris hid in the bows. He couldn't see Bosun and the others, as they were right underneath the boat. But he could see the gulls as they circled above, watching. Eventually the gulls swooped down and settled on the bulwarks where the ladder used to lean.

Doris was really impressed at the fight Madge and John had put up. He could feel his heart thumping with excitement.

"Gulls!" he spat with contempt, and silently crept along the deck. The gulls were staring fixedly at the ground below, ready to pounce on the nest robbers as soon as they appeared.

Doris crawled softly along the deck on his belly, eyes fixed on them, not even daring to breathe. He got closer and closer, and when he was right behind them, he pounced!

"*Gull! Gull!*" he yelled, sinking his teeth into one of them and clipping the other with his claws, yanking out a couple of tail feathers. The gulls shrieked and leapt into the air, feathers flying, screaming, "*CAT! CAT!*" They flew high into the sky and back to their nest.

White feathers swirled in the air and gently fell, settling on the ground below. After a while Bosun, John, Madge and Chippy peeked out from under the hull.

"I think they've gone!" said Bosun, straightening up.

"They can be bad, them seagulls," said Chippy, looking at the sky expectantly. "They got long memories, so I've heard. Like I said, my cousin had a problem with his for years."

John and Madge stood at the bottom of the ladder, looking at all the feathers lying around them on the ground.

Madge looked up to see where they had come from and saw Doris sitting on the bulwarks, lazily looking out over the estuary.

He was purring happily as if nothing had happened – but there was just a tiny feather caught in the corner of his mouth.

Then, almost as soon as Madge had seen him,
Doris was gone.

Over the next few weeks, every time the seagulls saw
Bosun, they would cry an alarm. Sometimes they
swooped out of the sky like fighter jets and pecked or
clawed at his head as they swept past. Bosun would
dive for cover and wave his hands in the air frantically
trying to bat them off.

A lot of the time they menaced him by circling overhead and spraying him with poo. The poo attack happened nearly everyday, and it seemed to Bosun that he would always be covered in bird guano. In the end he resigned himself to wearing his overalls all the time and just brushing off the worst of the dried poo, before climbing into them in the morning.

"The chicks will be old enough to fly soon, and that'll be the end of it then," Cap tried to reassure him, but Bosun wasn't convinced the seagulls would ever leave him alone. For the first time in his life he began to look forward to the rainy days – on rainy days there was no sign of the gulls and he could wear normal clothes.

The gulls never bothered Doris again. They only had it in for Bosun…

THE QUEEN

Doris was sitting on the bulwarks trying to spot where Jasper might be, when he saw the boatyard boss waving his arms at Bosun. As soon as he'd gone, Bosun started to tidy. Doris thought it was strange as he'd never seen Bosun tidy anything up before. He was wondering what might be happening to make Bosun clear everything away, when he heard Freda shouting from the other end of the yard. She raced down the yard towards him and flapped up the ladder with great speed. She was at the top in the blink of an eye.

"The Queen's here! The Queen's here!" she yelled, dancing around on the deck excitedly. John and Madge appeared immediately.

"The Queen's here!" shouted Freda, just in case they hadn't heard the first time.

"Who's the Queen?" asked Doris. "Do we need to hide again?" he added, anxiously thinking about the Beast.

"Not hide exactly," John said. "The Queen's the owner of the boatyard. He's not here very often. He's called the Queen 'cause he acts like the Queen. Everything has to be spick and span when he visits. He saunters about with his nose in the air and everything gets done for him. His pet is a horrible little spoilt dog that stays with him in the big house."

"He's not little, he's big!" corrected Madge.

John looked down at little Madge. "Bigger than you," he agreed with a smirk. Then he went on, frowning. "He's a violent little thug. He bit Bosun last time he was here."

"There he is!" shouted Freda, and they all turned to see Queen's pet on the balcony of the big house. Doris agreed he looked horrible and the thought of him biting Bosun made his blood boil. Queen's pet saw them all watching him and wrinkled up his nose, baring his grubby teeth in a sneering growl.

"Nice!" grunted John. "He hasn't changed for the better since his last visit."

"I hate Queen's pet, he's always trying to bite me," moaned Freda. "He's even worse than Jasper!"

"You're faster than him, though," said John smiling. "Anyway, he'll only be here for a couple of days. Let's just keep out of his way."

Doris looked across at the balcony where the ugly little Queen's pet was still snarling at them. Worse than Jasper? The idea made him tremble. Maybe staying in for the day wasn't such a bad idea.

That night Doris sat on the bulwarks and spent even longer searching the boatyard for any sign of Jasper. It was bad enough that he had that vicious monster to avoid, but now he had Queen's pet to worry about as well, so he also scoured the yard for him. But Queen's pet seemed to be safely tucked up in bed inside the big house. Only when he was absolutely sure it was clear did Doris venture down the ladder and into the shadows. Jasper had scented his territory – Doris could smell it; he'd even had the cheek to scent the bottom of Doris's ladder! It was obvious that Jasper was deadly serious about the boatyard belonging to him and wasn't going to let Doris have even a small part of it – not without a fight. Doris had no intention of getting caught by him, not after the last time – but after a whole day inside he needed to stretch his legs, so he decided to be extra sneaky about it. He was at least younger and faster than Jasper and, thanks to Madge, maybe Jasper would think twice about attacking him on the boat again.

Doris stayed close to *Prosperity*, just in case he needed to dash back, but he didn't see Jasper at all. Soon he started to venture a little further afield.

He'd just crept up to the corner of the big house when he smelt Jasper's fresh scent everywhere.

There was a lot of it over everything. Doris was crouching in the shadows, his heart pounding against his ribs, when the sound of a latch and a handle turning rang out in the silent night air. The door of the big house squeaked open, splashing the gravel drive with an electric beam of light. Queen's pet was out! Doris leapt to his feet and  ran as fast as he could down the yard and through the shadows. He raced up the ladder and jumped through a porthole to safety.

Bosun was the first one out of bed in the morning.

"Now the Queen's arrived, I'll never get anything done except tidying," he grumbled as he put on the kettle. "*Everything clean and tidy!*" he muttered to himself. Cap slid out of her bunk straight into her slippers.

"Has he brought his horrid little dog with him?" she asked, pulling on her thick cardigan.

"Yes. And if it bites me again I'll show it the end of my boot!" snapped Bosun.

After breakfast Doris sat with John and Madge on the deck. Doris had decided to try and get along better with Madge – to spend more time with her and get to know her. Madge had saved him from Jasper, and for that reason alone Doris knew she couldn't be all bad. And after all, John had insisted that she had a good side.

He watched idly as Freda made her way to Shipwright's boat; he always gave her a piece of toast when he was around. She was almost there when Doris heard a snapping bark, and before he could shout a warning, Queen's pet came running out of the big house and straight for Freda.

Freda squawked in alarm and started flapping in panic. She couldn't decide which way to run – back home was too far, while the Shipwright's boat was closer, but it was so high up. Could she make it? She didn't know what to do.

"Run!" shouted Doris, as Queen's pet raced across the yard towards Freda.

Hearing Freda's cries, John and Madge spun around.

"RUN!" they all shouted from high up on the deck.

They stood watching helplessly as Queen's pet dashed across the yard towards poor panicking Freda. Finally Freda ran for Shipwright's boat. She flapped and flapped to lift off the ground. Everyone gasped as Queen's pet leapt into the air to pounce on Freda. At that moment, Shipwright appeared and in one movement jumped off the deck and swooped Freda into his arms.

"Clear off, yer little thug!" he shouted, and Queen's pet skidded to a halt. The nasty creature backed away, snarling.

Shipwright bounced across the yard and up *Prosperity*'s ladder, popping Freda onto the deck next to them with a smile.

"I hate Queen's pet!" grunted Freda.

"Me too!" frowned Doris.

"He'll be gone again soon," reassured John as he gave Freda a soothing lick.

A SAD DAY IN THE BOATYARD

Doris was stuck on the boat, watching the comings and goings of the yard. He hadn't even managed to get out during the night because Queen's pet had been out until late, and then as soon as he'd gone to bed, Jasper had been on the prowl. Doris had given up and gone to sleep, but by the time he woke up, so had Queen's pet.

Queen's pet was now sitting outside the boatyard

office door, snapping at everyone trying to get in and out. He'd even attacked Shipwright when he had ventured within range, in revenge for saving Freda from his attack.

As Doris watched Shipwright wading to his anchored dinghy to bail it out, he regretted staying for his breakfast and missing the opportunity to get out before Queen's pet was at large. When he was just waking up at dawn, he'd heard Freda flap down the ladder. He wished he'd gone with her.

It was midmorning before Queen's pet eventually went inside the house, but as soon as he had, Doris saw Jasper sneaking under the boat. Doris was beside himself – he'd never get off the boat if this kept up!

Jasper had stopped at the quay and was watching Shipwright pulling at a heap of fishing nets as the tide ebbed away. He found a way down to the freshly exposed seabed and was picking his way carefully along the mud to avoid the puddles. Doris sat on the bulwarks and watched him approach the heap of tangled netting and seaweed that had interested Shipwright. He sniffed the pile and looked directly up at Doris.

"Have you lot been throwing your rubbish in the sea?" Jasper sneered down his nose and strode off as if he was the king of the yard. Doris bristled.

He squinted at the mound, but couldn't make out what it was. He decided to go down and take a closer look, but Shipwright was climbing up the ladder and blocking his way.

Shipwright knocked on the wheelhouse door.

Doris thought he looked hunched and shrunken. He wasn't smiling like he usually did, and his eyes were red and swollen as if he'd been crying. He leant forward and whispered into Bosun's ear. Doris watched them with a growing sense of doom as they climbed down the ladder, down the quay wall and onto the seabed. They picked a path to the heap of fishing net.

Silently they stood and stared at it. Doris didn't want to take a closer look any more, but he couldn't help it. Maybe it was just some rubbish caught in the net?

Bosun and Shipwright untangled whatever it was and stood up, eyes fixed on what they had in their hands. Shipwright pulled a hessian sack out of his pocket and they put the object into it.

They talked for a long time, standing on the mud, until the last remaining tide ebbed out of the estuary, leaving only a stream flowing seawards.

Doris knew, the moment they climbed back up the ladder. He could smell past the old sack and its tar and oil odours, past the pungency of fish scales and seaweed that soaked into the sack, to the body that Bosun and Shipwright had recovered from the fishing net. He could smell Freda like he always could, like nothing had changed. She smelt the same as she had that very morning, only she wasn't moving. As he watched the sack go past, he knew things would never be the same again. The sea had killed Freda silently; no one had seen or heard it take her. Shipwright had only found her when the waves dumped her onto the mud.

John and Madge came and sat beside Doris. They didn't say a thing. They didn't need to: they could smell past the sack, the tar, the oil, the fish scales and the seaweed, too.

Bosun and Cap picked a spot in a green corner of the boatyard. Bosun dug a deep hole and Cap placed the cotton sack gently into it. Shipwright placed a large stone at the head and stood back, looking intently at the grave.

Somebody came and solemnly placed a biscuit next to the sack; someone else added a piece of cake.

Soon people from all over the boatyard appeared and added things to Freda's grave. Shipwright wasn't the only one with tears in his eyes. By the end of the afternoon, when finally the grave was covered, there were more people stood there than Doris had ever seen in one place. Only the Queen and Queen's pet were strangely absent.

The crowd thinned and dispersed. Cap and Bosun wandered home and finally John, Madge and Doris were the only ones left at the graveside.

It was all so sudden, that not one of them could quite believe they would never see Freda again. Somehow she would come charging back into the yard and everything would be the same again…but they knew in their hearts it couldn't happen. She was gone for good.

JOHN

The day after Freda's funeral, everyone felt numb. There was no chatting over breakfast or making small talk. Doris had decided that Queen's pet must have had something to do with Freda's death, even though no one had actually seen him chase her into the sea. He had mentioned as much to John and Madge and they had agreed. John was especially upset. He kept looking into Freda's house in case it was all a dream and nothing had really happened.

"You miss her, don't you?" Bosun said, stroking John's head.

When Bosun climbed down the ladder to work with Chippy, Cap winched John and Madge down as well, to cheer them up and take their minds off Freda. She knew they liked to mess about in the yard, and they  had been stuck on the boat the whole time that the Queen had been in residence. He didn't like mess or anyone else's dogs, or noise, or boats – or people, for that matter. So when he was around everyone stayed in and waited until he was gone.

Now things were different. Freda was dead, the dogs were upset and Bosun had work to do. John could help by keeping Queen's pet from biting him.

But John wasn't only sad – he was also very, very angry.

John knew in his heart that Queen's pet was to blame. He might not have seen him chase Freda into the sea, but deep down, he was sure that was what had happened. *Prosperity* wasn't in the water any more, so Freda couldn't have just fallen in – she must have been chased.

Doris couldn't believe his luck – neither Jasper nor Queen's pet would trouble him now, not with John and Madge around. He leapt down the ladder to join them, but as soon as his paws touched the ground, Queen's pet appeared in front of the house.

Doris froze for a moment as Queen's pet sneered in his direction, but the moment passed and Doris reassured himself that he was safe.

Doris rubbed up against John's leg and was surprised how rigid it was. Looking up he saw that John was as still as a statue, every muscle tense, like a coiled spring, staring at the horrid little dog.

Doris looked at Queen's pet strolling across the gravel as though nothing had happened.

Suddenly John sprang into action.

One minute he was as still as stone – the next he was tearing at full speed across the yard straight for Queen's pet.

Doris noticed the little dog's face turn from sneering hatred to absolute terror as John bore down on him. He turned and fled, with John in hot pursuit. Madge was right behind him, shouting excitedly, "Go on John, get him! Let's get him!"

Bosun spun around. "JOHN!" he shouted at the top of his voice.

But John's hatred had boiled over and blood was pounding through his veins. All he could see was the back end of the horrid little dog that had killed Freda, getting nearer and nearer.

"JOHN!" Cap shouted from the deck.

"JOHN!" Shipwright shouted.

Everyone from all over the yard started shouting and running after John, desperately trying to stop him, but when John heard the shouting it sounded like a crowd cheering him on. "John! JOHN! *JOHN!*"

John was a leap away and he launched into the air for his closing attack, his teeth bared in a frightening snarl, foam spraying from his jaws. He lunged forward to land squarely on the snivelling little dog, but suddenly Queen's pet leapt desperately off the quay, and in a second hit the water with a splash.

John skidded to a halt at the edge, frothing at the mouth, hackles raised in anger and excitement. He barked and barked and barked at being cheated of his revenge. Madge was barking beside him too.

"Come back 'ere! We're gonna get you!" Madge shouted after the little dog. Queen's pet swam as fast as he could away from John and Madge, out into deep water.

Doris stood as still as a statue throughout the entire episode. He watched as John and Madge were surrounded by everyone from the yard. He was completely shaken by what had just happened. He had never thought John could be so scary – he had always thought of him as gentle giant.

The Queen strode out of the house, shouting at Bosun and the others, pointing at John. Madge started barking and snapping at him and everyone was shouting and waving

their arms about. The Queen tried to shake Madge free as she tugged at his trouser leg. John strained against his collar, but Bosun had a tight hold and pulled him away. Panting like a mad beast, steam puffing out of his nostrils and mouth, John was led back to *Prosperity*. Madge bounded alongside, still enthusiastically encouraging him like a boxer's ringside trainer.

The Queen called to his pet, but the little dog carried on swimming away in frightened panic.

Doris, still rooted to the spot, stared at John approaching. Gradually his panting became breathing, his fur fell limp on his back and his old friendly features returned to his face. By the time Cap winched him back on the boat, John was his old kindly self.

Eventually Shipwright rowed out to bring Queen's pet back.

Doris watched the Queen put him in his car with the rest of his stuff, waving his arms about and shouting at the boatyard boss. He kept pointing angrily at *Prosperity*, too. Then he got into the car and drove away.

As the Queen's car disappeared in a cloud of dust, a big growling truck trundled down the yard past it. They all stared. Doris retreated to his safe place under the bed. He could still hear the growling truck, but the noise of it was much more distant from his cosy den. He curled up in a tight ball hoping this truck didn't mean any more bad things were going to happen. He'd had quite enough for one day.

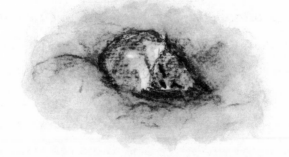

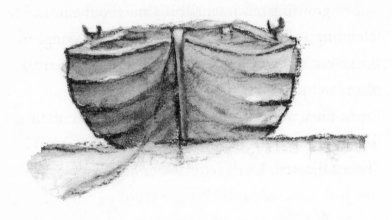

ALL INSIDE OUT

When Doris woke up that afternoon, he could sense
that his whole world had changed again. He pushed
his way out of his den and into the cabin. There were
people working on the back of the boat, ripping large
parts off. They had already taken the roof off.
Skipping past all the boots and tools, he found that
outside wasn't any better. The sound of electric tools
buzzed loudly in his ears as he tried to weave a path

through the comings and goings of all the workmen.

The growling truck sat silently next to the boat. He felt a surge of relief as he spotted John and Madge in the green corner of the boatyard, near Freda's resting place, and picked his way through the legs to join them. They were looking a lot less bewildered than he felt. John was on a long rope that was tied to an old disused dinghy.

"Why are you on a rope?" asked Doris.

"I can't be trusted anymore," John explained, hanging his head.

"He's a dope on a rope," smirked Madge.

Every day after that brought the same noise and bustle, with people coming and going, but Doris didn't mind because he was happy to spend his mornings under the bed and his afternoons with John and Madge, watching the activities on *Prosperity* from a safe distance. He found a perfect place in the cover of the dinghy that John was tied to; it stretched over its length and was like a hammock, just right for him to laze about in the sun and snooze.

It was a new experience for him, outside in the sun, knowing John and Madge would keep him safe from Jasper.

The only time he saw Cap and Bosun was at breakfast and dinner times; the rest of the time they were busy on the boat. The green corner became an oasis of tranquillity for Doris. Even when he went out on his nightly jaunts, the green corner was safe. Jasper never ventured into it. Doris decided it must have been the overpowering smell of John that kept him away. Doris had never felt so free from Jasper before, and he loved it.

Each day they went back to the boat for their dinner and saw the insides changing: varnish, paint, new windows and even cushions – until it started to feel like a proper home again. All the paintwork sparkled and the cushions were soft and colourful. Soon, one by one, the workmen disappeared.

The day the growling truck came back, Doris was sitting with John and Madge by the dinghy. It was much bigger and louder than the other truck. John and Madge sat happily and watched as the monster belched smoke and raised its crane above *Prosperity*, but it terrified Doris and he crept under the dinghy and peeked out from a gap in the cover. After a lot of shouting over the noise of the roaring engine, the monster swung *Prosperity* high up into the air and then back into the water.

Long after the crane had gone, Doris, John and Madge ventured back onto the boat. It was back on the quay where it had been before, the waves lapping the hull as the boat bobbed about on the sea.

"We'll be chugging soon!" said Bosun, rubbing his hands together excitedly.

"We have to be!" Cap reminded him.

"Indeed!" said Bosun, remembering the boatyard boss's explicit instructions to be gone before the Queen's return.

It had taken them a long time to get *Prosperity* mended and make it a seaworthy boat. *Prosperity* had never been good enough to go to sea. It had been towed when they had first brought it to the boatyard. Now it was ready to leave under its own steam.

"I'm ready for somewhere new," said Cap looking out across the estuary.

"Me too!" smiled Bosun.

As night fell Doris strode around the deck. He was a lot bigger than he had been the last time the boat was in the water. He sat on the bulwarks and looked over the side of the boat at the sea that had taken Freda.

He didn't like the water any more: it frightened him. It was inky black and its slurping noises made it even more threatening. It was as if the sea was waiting for him to slip and tumble into its blackness, so it could take him, too.

A fish jumped just below him and Doris flinched.

John and Madge joined him on the deck. The smell of fresh varnish wafted around them. Sitting listening to the echoey sounds of the estuary should have been relaxing, but it wasn't – they were all tense.

No one said anything, but each one of them had a growing feeling that something was about to change – something big.

A MONSTER GROWLS

Doris froze in absolute terror. He had never, ever felt such panic before. The sound of alarm beeps and a rattling roar consumed the whole boat. He crouched in terror in the main cabin, frozen to the spot, the growling grumbling noise screaming all around him. Every inch of his body was tense and shouted at him to flee, but he couldn't. He saw things in snapshot images. John wide-eyed, tail between his legs and shaking.

Madge, wildly pacing back and forth, like a goldfish in a tiny bowl desperately looking for a way out. Cap, holding onto the wheel up in the wheelhouse, peering out of the front window on tiptoe; and Bosun grinning, all black and sooty, wiping his oily hands and beaming a triumphant smile from below in the engine room, where the noise was coming from.

Suddenly Doris found he could move and he raced as fast as he could under the bed.

He was still surrounded by the noise of the monster growling, but at least it was a little muffled. Everything vibrated from the rumbling, but in here he felt safer. He couldn't imagine what could make such a terrifying noise, or why Bosun and Cap seemed so happy about it. It must be the biggest monster in the whole world, he thought. He tried not to think about what it would do to him if it caught him and worried whether John and Madge were all right. In the end he decided he had to know and gingerly crept from his hidey-hole into the cabin cupboard. He couldn't see the monster anywhere. It was still in the dark engine room, but he could see everyone else and was thankful and relieved they were all still OK.

Cap and Bosun were thrilled to bits. They were smiling from ear to ear. John and Madge were sitting stiffly in the middle of the cabin floor. They didn't look at all happy.

"We're ready," Bosun shouted over the noise, smiling.

"Mmmm, now just the sea and the weather to worry about!" frowned Cap, her smile gone.

"But just think, we can go anywhere now, across the sea to where it's hot and sunny!" he beamed.

"I know. I'm excited about going places, but crossing the sea terrifies me," she yelled over the din. Then her whole face brightened as though the sun had just broken out from the clouds. "Party first!" she smiled and jumped back up to the wheelhouse.

As soon as Cap went up the stairs, the noise stopped. Doris waited, hardly daring to breathe and hoping with all his heart it wouldn't start again. When he was absolutely sure the growling was over, he jumped cautiously out of the cupboard and onto the cabin floor.

From the moment the noise stopped, everyone returned to normal, as though nothing had happened. John and Madge were happily chatting; Cap and Bosun were enjoying a cup of coffee and a biscuit.

Everything was relaxed and peaceful.

Doris joined them in the cabin, feeling a little bruised from the noise and darting the odd glance into the darkness of the engine room to make sure that the monster had been completely put to sleep.

THE PARTY

Doris was pleased to get out into the fresh night air of
the boatyard. He still felt shaken by the monster
experience. He cautiously kept an eye out for Jasper,
but with so much activity in this corner of the yard,
he knew Jasper would probably keep away. Bosun and
Cap were making a bonfire not far from the boat and
John and Madge were running and playing around it.
They had put out tables with lots of food and drink

on them, and soon Madge and John took up residence there, waiting for any titbits to come their way.

Lots of people started to arrive, bringing many different musical instruments and more food. Soon the party was underway and the music lifted in the

air and floated across the boatyard. Doris sat in the shadows, away from the glow of the party. He'd found a place up on a small boat, far away from all the hubbub, outside the ring of oil lamps that were on poles stuck into the ground. He sat and watched the comings and goings. The chatter and laughter. Madge and John's endless munching. He liked to be distant from it all, rather than in the thick of it.

As the evening wore on, the crowd thinned. Now there was just a small group in a circle around the bonfire – mainly people who lived in the yard.

Someone was juggling with flaming rags on sticks, while a few in the circle beat drums, and people danced.

Chippy was happily playing with John. He threw a ball and John leapt after it. They had been playing the game for some time. John loved to chase ball, but Chippy started to look tired. "Last one now!" he told John, and threw the ball as hard as he could.

The ball bounced away from the fire, followed closely by John. It bounced over an oil lamp and into the dark. John chased it excitedly.

Doris gasped in horror as he saw the scene unfold in front of him. The ball, the flaming lamp, John jumping and hitting the lamp. Doris froze. Suddenly John was ablaze! Flames licked up his leg and surrounded his head. Doris gaped in disbelief.

John was a ball of flames, running and barking in
panic, the air feeding the flames as they flickered into
the night.

Bosun screamed John's name. Cap cried out.
Chippy leapt up and grabbed John as he ran
panicking in circles around him. He smothered John
completely with his coat, and as fast as it had
happened, the flames were gone.

Doris still couldn't breathe. Everyone ran towards
John and surrounded him, so Doris couldn't see if he
was all right. Suddenly, Cap laughed out loud and
Bosun smiled.

Doris remembered to
breathe again as John leapt
out of the group wagging his
tail. The only sign that
anything had happened was
that the fur around his neck
was a bit shorter.

Doris felt dizzy, but his
body relaxed with a wave of exhaustion. Bosun put all
the oil lamps out.

Cap and Bosun hugged John. They'd checked him
over for any burns, but he was fine. It was amazing
that he had come out of it unhurt.

"I can't bear to think what could have happened if
you hadn't caught him when you did!" Cap said,
clutching Chippy by his arms. "Thank you so much!"

"He was too fast for me, I couldn't get to him," said
Bosun, hugging John, not wanting to ever let go.
"Thanks!"

"It was just lucky," Chippy said, shaking his head.
Everyone gradually dispersed back to their own boats.

Cap and Bosun couldn't wait to get the dogs back to the safety of *Prosperity*.

"It happened so fast," Cap murmured as she climbed down onto the boat. All the colour had drained from her face.

Doris stretched in the silent still night air of the empty yard. He loved this time of night, when he was the only one moving about and the whole yard was his. He strode along the pathway that wound its way through the boats propped up on the hard. He sneaked under tarpaulins and piles of wood, pounced on moths fluttering in the night breeze and stalked imaginary prey through the shadows. He was hiding under the party table, poking his head out of the tablecloth that draped to the floor, when he smelt the scent of Jasper.

He looked across the empty expanse between him and *Prosperity*. It was a long way. There was nothing in between, nothing to sneak behind, nothing to hide him – only a gaping space where the party had been.

Jasper would attack him before he ever got to the other side. Doris stiffened. His leg throbbed at the memory of it being ripped open. Suddenly he felt like a little scared kitten again, all alone in the dark.

THE SHOWDOWN

Doris squatted, hunched by the misery of it all. Then he saw something – something white – Jasper!

He relaxed a little because at least he knew where Jasper was hiding now. Even though he couldn't see him properly, he knew in an instant it was him. The overpowering scent and that little patch of white poking out from behind a post could mean nothing else.

Doris ducked into the shadows, and, keeping out of Jasper's sight, silently crept around to where he was hidden. He could smell how close Jasper was.

Doris trembled, fighting an overwhelming urge to run away. He slowly crawled inch by inch towards his fear, as if Jasper was a magnet pulling him in.

Ever since he had come to live in the yard, Jasper had been such a huge part of his life. Although he hadn't seen him since Freda died, and had only been attacked by him once, the fear of him, his scent, his presence, was always lurking in the darkest corners. Every time he set his paws off the boat, he had expected Jasper to be there. He had been completely dominated by the fear of Jasper and what he could do to him. Doris was terrified as he silently crept towards him. What if Jasper smelt his scent? Did Jasper know that he was here?

He was close now. He hid behind a plank of wood. He could hear Jasper breathing. Hesitantly he peeked out, holding his breath, not daring to make the tiniest movement that would him give away.

Jasper was right there, sitting side on, not a cat's length between them. Doris stared in disbelief at this white cat that had terrorised him for what felt like his whole life. He straightened as utter astonishment took hold and he saw how tiny and old this monster actually was. No longer a huge, terrifying bully, but an old shrunken cat, now much smaller than Doris.

For Doris had grown into a large, strong tomcat –
he had outgrown Jasper in every way. When he had
seen him on the seabed it had been from far above on
Prosperity, and he'd looked just as huge from there.
Doris stopped hiding and sat, feeling confused. How
could this be the same monster?

"You're *Jasper*?" he heard himself ask, even though
he knew it was – Jasper's scent was unmistakable.
After all, he'd avoided it for so long.

"This is my yard!" said Jasper, in a dismissive tone,
but he didn't look round. He just kept staring into the
distance like an old king sweeping an underling aside.

"Yeah, but I share it now," Doris replied.

"Ha! You still think you have a home," Jasper
turned to sneer at him. "I had one once. I lived
on a superyacht.
Nothing like that leaky
old tub you inhabit!
They'll never take you!
You'll be left behind, just
like I was."

"Take me where?" Doris asked, feeling puzzled by this turn of the conversation.

"Nowhere, you idiot! That's the point – it's what sailors do. They'll leave you behind. Then it'll just be you and me. Cats don't travel." Jasper smiled a nasty, mocking smile. "But this is my yard, got it? I had to fight for it and now it's all *mine*!"

Doris slunk back to *Prosperity*. What was the point of reasoning with grumpy Jasper? He knew now that he was just a mad old cat talking rubbish. *Wasn't he?*

Doris curled up on his cushion, but he couldn't sleep. Jasper's words kept tumbling about in his mind. He should have been overjoyed that Jasper was no longer a threat, but he wasn't. He squeezed his eyes shut, trying to convince himself that his family would never leave him.

LEAVING

It was just before dawn when Chippy, the crane driver, Shipwright and all the other people that lived on boats in the yard started to arrive at the quay. Cap stood at the wheel looking very nervous. Bosun was in the engine room.

Doris was puzzled by all the activity. He had just got back from his nightly wanderings. He had gone out again after giving up on sleep, knowing he could

potter about and Jasper could do nothing to stop him.
But he was still haunted by Jasper's poisonous words
as he sat patiently waiting for his breakfast. He stood
in the cabin and wondered what could be going
on. Madge and John paced nervously up and down
the deck. Bosun came out of the engine room
looking tired.

"Ahh, there you are!"
he said, sweeping Doris
off his paws and popping
him down in the
bedroom. "You're best off
in here," he said with a
nervous smile, and
disappeared.

Then the dreaded
alarm beeps sounded from
the wheelhouse. Doris felt
the fur on his back rise
and the monster coughed and spluttered before it
roared into life. The whole boat vibrated. He looked

up and saw that a porthole was open. Panicking, he was outside and jumping free of *Prosperity* before anyone had time to see him.

He crept under a tarpaulin covering a dinghy on the quay. It was only when he was hidden that he relaxed and watched from a safe distance. The roar of the monster was much quieter from his hiding place and he felt very pleased with himself. He had had time to think about his escape route and where he would hide. The last time the monster was awake it had utterly shaken him, and being trapped and terrified inside the boat had made it so much worse. He had decided then that if it ever woke up again he would find a way to get off the boat. Doris relaxed and licked his paws, smiling to himself. He had escaped the monster – his plan had worked!

There was a cheer from the crowd on the quay when the engine started. There was nothing like seeing someone you'd watched working on a boat for months finally taking it out to sea. For everyone who lived in the damp and cold, banging in nails and painting, replacing planks and wondering if they would ever see their own boat float again, it was a real boost. All the people looking at *Prosperity* were really thinking about what their own boat would look like, how they would feel at the wheel and how their engine would growl one day.

John and Madge paced the deck, occasionally stopping to get patted by Chippy or Shipwright.

"Where's Doris?" John asked.

"Bosun put him under the bed," Madge replied. "He's hiding. I don't blame him."

Doris peeked out from underneath the tarpaulin. He could see John and Madge on the deck through the legs of the onlookers. He was relieved to see the monster hadn't harmed them and felt smug about finding his new hiding place.

"I'll get the ropes," Bosun said as he jumped off the boat. Chippy and Shipwright slapped him on the back and wished him good luck. John and Madge started barking with excitement as he untied the ropes and threw them on the deck. He jumped smartly back on the boat and beamed a huge smile. Cap tried not to look nervous as she drove the boat slowly away from the quay.

Doris watched Bosun untie the ropes. He watched John and Madge barking excitedly. None of it worried him…until he saw the boat move! All of a sudden he realised why the ropes were there – to keep the boat against the quay! He had never thought of *Prosperity* moving without a crane.

He cried out as loud as he could, but his voice was no match against the growl of the monster.

He stood staring at *Prosperity* as it moved further from the yard, chugging out into the deep water, getting smaller and smaller as it went out into the bay.

He could hardly make out the figures of John, Madge and Bosun on the deck as the boat followed the curve of the bay and finally disappeared behind the headland.

Doris hunched up, still
not believing what had
just happened. He
sat, consumed
with the misery of
it all, still staring at the
spot where *Prosperity* had disappeared from view. They
were gone. They had left him behind: everything he
had known had disappeared. His family, his home and
the best friends he'd ever had – all gone. Doris began

to cry. If only he'd stayed under the
bed! Jasper had been right all along. If
only he'd listened!

He felt a presence behind him. "I
told you!" Jasper hissed unpleasantly.
"Cats and travelling don't mix."

Doris stared at the old weather-beaten cat. He
thought about how Jasper had been left behind by his
family, too. Is that what had made him so bitter?

"They won't come back," Jasper went on, "and you
can't stay here. This is my yard!"

Doris was too upset to argue with Jasper. He felt so utterly alone that even Jasper's harsh words were strangely comforting. Jasper hadn't gone so there was at least something left of his old life. But Doris's whole world had changed. If he was no longer a ship's cat, what was he to be? He couldn't be a yard cat, either, because Jasper was that already.

"I've nowhere else to go," he whispered almost to himself, not wanting to believe it but realising it was true. He felt devastated. He longed for John. He'd know what to do, he'd sort it out. But John was gone, along with Doris's old life.

Doris felt utterly lost.

"Well, well!" Jasper sneered. "I guess I could use a slave."

Doris looked into Jasper's twisted face. Doris's spirit had left him, any spark of his bright personality dulled. He felt completely numb.

Then in the distance, he heard the sound of a monster – the very same monster that had filled him with absolute terror. But not this time! Now it lifted his heart, it was music to his ears! There was *Prosperity*, shining in the sunlight, chugging around the bay towards him.

There were John and Madge on board, barking and barking.

"Doris!" shouted Bosun as he jumped onto the quay and scooped him up in his arms. He held Doris level with his eyes in both of his strong hands. Doris looked into Bosun's beaming face. His kind eyes were all watery. Doris purred and purred.

"You scared the living daylights out of us! We thought we'd lost you! The ship's not a ship without the ship's cat, and what a big ship's cat you are!"

Bosun smiled and hugged him all the way to the boat, which was waiting on the quay.

He felt safe in the strong arms of Bosun and the growl of the monster now sounded even sweeter than before.

"You've found him!" cried Cap.

John and Madge jumped up and licked him all over.

"Oh, Doris!" said John, licking his face. Bosun put Doris down on the chart table next to him.

"Come on, the tide is going out, we'll have to be quick!" Cap insisted as she stroked Doris's head.

Once again Bosun jumped down to cast off the ropes. He gave Jasper a farewell stroke. Doris sat in the wheelhouse and John nuzzled him, not wanting to let him out of his sight. Cap steered off the quay and out into the bay. Doris looked over John's head at sad old Jasper getting smaller and smaller, until they turned behind the headland and Jasper disappeared for good.

Bosun took Doris
down below, past the
growling monster
and into the
bedroom.

"You stay here where it's
safe," said Bosun. "I'll call you when we get there."

Doris curled up in his favourite place under the
bed. The monster was growling in the background,
the boat swayed in the waves, and he was so glad to be
home. He had his family back.

He was Ship's Cat Doris and he couldn't be happier.

Look out for

Beryl
Goes
Wild

Turn the page to read an extract!

MEETING THE WILD SIDE

A twig cracked nearby.

"Are you all right?" said a small voice.

Beryl looked around. She couldn't see anyone.

Out of the foliage stepped a scruffy little animal.
Beryl blinked at it, trying to work out what it was.
The creature was very muddy, with a pointed snout
at one end and a curly tail at the other. Under all
the brown, straw-like hair and caked-on mud, it

looked like a kind of pig.

Beryl's heart thumped hard against her ribcage as she realised what this strange creature must be.

A wild pig!

"Don't eat me!" Beryl cried.

"Why ever would I eat you?" asked the wild pig. "I saw you fall from the lorry. My name's Amber."

"I'm lost!" squeaked Beryl, as Amber came nearer. Beryl towered above her. She hadn't imagined that wild pigs would be so little. Beryl stretched her whole body upwards, to show Amber how much larger she really was.

"You can come home with me if you want. My Uncle Bert will know what to do," said Amber.

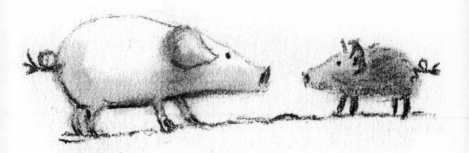

Beryl snorted. She didn't like that idea at all. If Gruff was right, she could catch something nasty from the wild pigs, or even end up as dinner.

What if that creature with the incredibly long ears came back and attacked her? Then her tummy rumbled – she was starving! She felt maybe she had no choice but to go home with Amber.

"OK," she said, and smiled nervously at her.

Beryl followed the wild pig, keeping her distance so it would be hard for Amber to try any funny business. As she stumbled along the track she kept stopping and looking around. She had seen a bit of the outside through the cracks in her sty, but actually being out in it was very strange.

"Who put all these trees here?" asked Beryl.

"I don't know. I think they've always been here," said Amber.

"It's very dirty," said Beryl. "Doesn't anybody ever sweep up?"

"Like who?" said Amber.

"The farmer?" said Beryl,

"Yeah, right!" snorted Amber.

Beryl didn't want to make this wild pig angry, so she changed the subject.

"How far is it to your uncle's home?" she wheezed. "I've never walked this far before and I'm getting very tired. The ground's got far too many lumps and bumps. Why isn't it flat?" She collapsed on the ground, huffing and puffing.

Amber frowned. "You can still see where we started from," she said. She began to wonder if she'd made a mistake helping this pork pig, but curiosity had got the better of her. She'd never seen or spoken to a pork pig before, though she'd heard stories about them from the other wild pigs. She'd always thought that they would be bigger, somehow. "You'll get used to it," she assured Beryl.

"Who put all these flowers here?" Beryl asked.

"Same person as the trees, I guess," Amber said with a giggle. She noticed how Beryl was looking around at everything, as if she had never seen trees or flowers before.

"Try sniffing one. It's a lily," Amber said gently.

"Sniff it?" said Beryl. "But why? What does it smell of?"

"Try it," Amber encouraged.

Beryl pulled herself up and edged around the flower. When she was safely facing Amber, with the flower between them, she gave it a quick sniff.

The smell was strong yet soft; it was summer; it was spring; it was the most wonderful smell Beryl had ever smelt. She shut her eyes and took a long, deep breath of it. At last she looked up at Amber with a delighted smile. Amber giggled.

"Do they all smell like that?" Beryl asked.

"They're all a bit different," said Amber.

The pink ones smelt sweet and the blue were
really faint and delicate. Some of them hardly had
any smell at all – Beryl had to bury her nose deep
into them and give a really big sniff. Others she
could smell long before she got to them.

Beryl forgot how tired and hungry she felt. She
pottered happily along the path behind Amber,
sniffing flowers to the left and to the right. She was
so happy she began to sing as she sniffed.

"Sunny day,
Being so free,
I love flowers,
They're so pongee."

"What's that?" asked Amber.

"Oh, nothing," said Beryl, going pink.

Amber stared. She had never ever seen a pig go pink before, and Beryl went seriously crimson.

"Tell me, please! I really liked it," said Amber.

"I made it up, but I'm not a very good singer," said Beryl, clearing her throat. "But I'll teach it to you, if you like."

After a few attempts, Amber joined in. Then she made up a second verse. Together Beryl and Amber walked along the path singing and sniffing flowers, towards Amber's home and Uncle Bert. And Beryl completely forgot how tired and hungry and scared she was.

"Sunny day,
Being so free,
I love flowers,
They're so pongee.
Tiddly tee,
Tiddly tum,
A walk in the woods
Is so much fun."

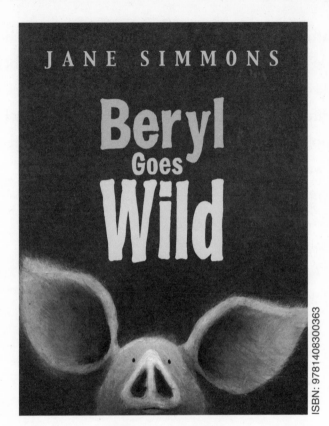